FRIENDS OF EARTH

5 STORIES TO TEACH SUSTAINABILITY

NIVEDITA

Copyright © Nivedita
All Rights Reserved.

This book has been published with all efforts taken to make the material error-free after the consent of the author. However, the author and the publisher do not assume and hereby disclaim any liability to any party for any loss, damage, or disruption caused by errors or omissions, whether such errors or omissions result from negligence, accident, or any other cause.

While every effort has been made to avoid any mistake or omission, this publication is being sold on the condition and understanding that neither the author nor the publishers or printers would be liable in any manner to any person by reason of any mistake or omission in this publication or for any action taken or omitted to be taken or advice rendered or accepted on the basis of this work. For any defect in printing or binding the publishers will be liable only to replace the defective copy by another copy of this work then available.

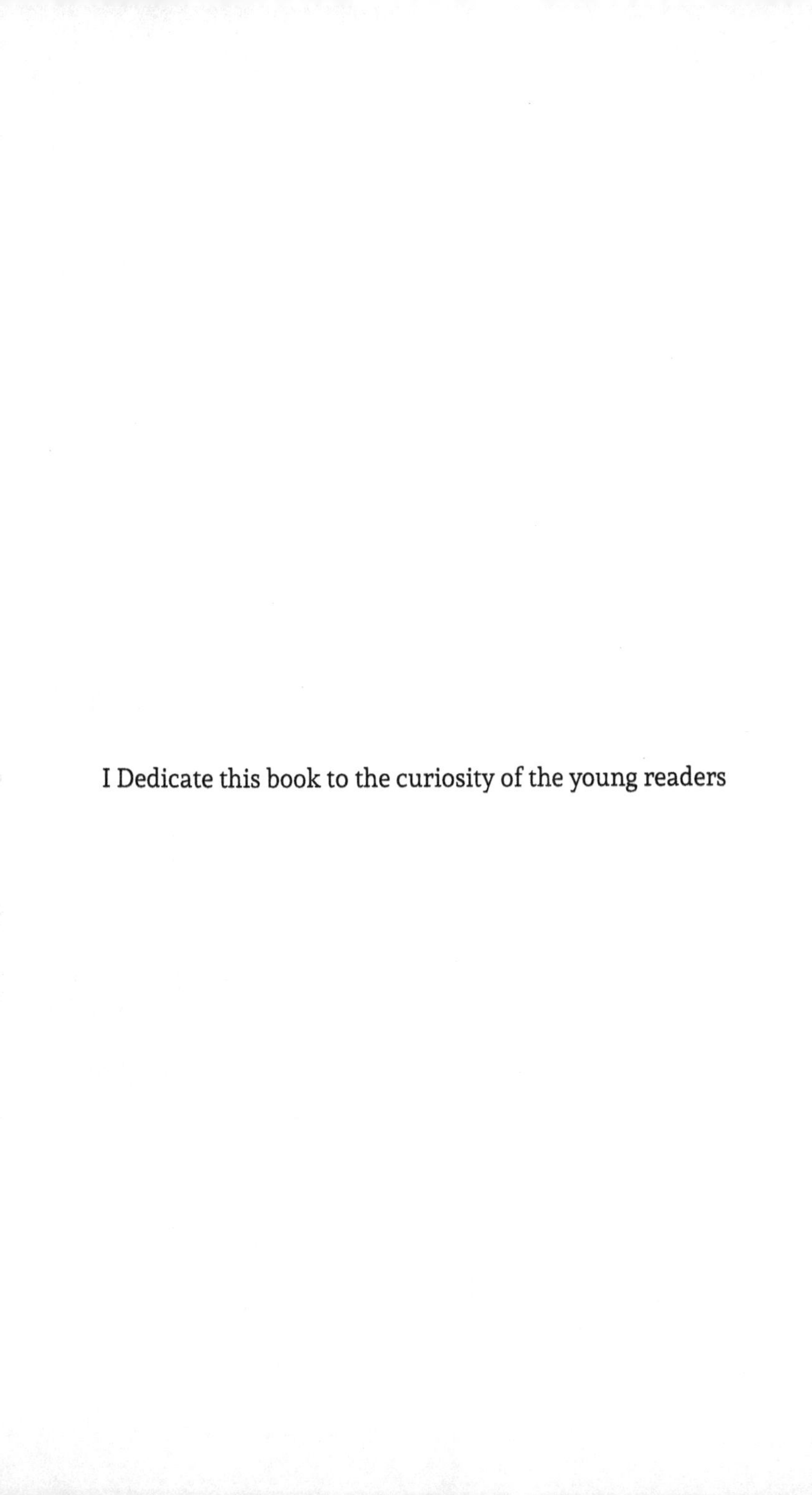

I Dedicate this book to the curiosity of the young readers

Contents

Preface   *vii*

1. 5 Stories To Teach Sustainability   1

Preface

The kids of present era deserve to hear more than the age old classic tales. The inquisitive nature of kids should not be stopped with just fairy tales. The intelligence and creativity in them must be appreciated by providing them with stories that goes with the reality of the current world.

I have created stories that would teach them about the society they live in. It would make them think about the past, present and the future of the earth we live in. The stories will help the adults and kids to act right.

Thanks

Have a productive read

Nivedita A

ONE

5 STORIES TO TEACH SUSTAINABILITY

1. Amma... when will god show a way to go to Mars?

Riah yelled, "*Pranith! Pack your bags and get ready, it is late for school*".

Pranith was lost in his thoughts. He didn't care about the words of Riah. Riah went near Pranith's room and yelled again." *Pranith, It is late, you will be punished if you are late. Please, pack up and get ready*". Pranith wrote a few lines that were pending in his assignment on global warming and packed his bag. He turned and looked at Riah as he packed. He said, "*Amma, I was thoughtful and worried about how we would survive on this earth.*" Pranith munched the sandwiches and left home with a question to Riah.When he was about to leave he said, "*Amma I just wrote in my science project that earth is losing its sustainability, and future generations will have a hard time living here.*" After that, he asked in a jocular way, "*Amma, When will god show the way to go to mars?*"

He asked the question and ran fast on hearing the horn of his school bus. Riah was moved by the matured thoughts of her son. She is an engineer working at ISRO. She always dreamt of flying to other planets. But, the question of her son made her thoughtful. She realized the mistakes that are made by adults. She had an hour to leave for work. She took her diary to look at the agenda. She saw that she had some pending works that must be checked regarding the lunar mission to be held in 5 years. Riah thought," Are we so fascinated about things in space and other planets that we forget to save our earth?" She thought to herself," Why should Pranith ask about going to mars?" why didn't he ask about the ways to make the earth sustainable?". The hour went fast and she shut the door of her home and drove to work.

It was sharp 10 A.M. The chief engineer called Riah to enquire about the lunar mission. Riah was breaking her head over the question asked by Pranith. Riah went into the chief engineer's room after she was ready with her data and the presentation. The question of Pranith was still on her head. The chief engineer looked at Riah and asked," *Riah, how is the work related to the lunar mission going on?*" Riah's mind was engrossed with the question of her son. She said, "*Sir, It is all most going to be done.*" *We would make a successful mission to Mars soon*". The chief engineer was perplexed. He exclaimed, "*Mars*". Riah realized her mistake, and said, "*Sorry sir, it was a slip of tongue.*" *My son asked about mars this morning, and I was thinking about it*". The chief engineer smiled and said, "*Riah, please have your mind on the official work as you step into ISRO*". He also said, "*Riah, please don't let the rocket into mars instead of the moon*". The chief engineer laughed after saying that. Riah left his room with a sheepish smile on realizing the blunt mistake that she made. She wanted to ask the chief engineer a question, but she didn't because she was trained to do what is said and never question. She wished to ask," *what is the lunar mission going to do for the earth?" Is it going to make the earth sustainable or is it going to prevent any natural calamity?*" Her mind was just engrossed in the thoughts of her son. She just walked out to have a break.

Riah always dreamt of flying to space, but she never got a chance. Riah wondered if she could take up a rocket and fly to Mars. The work on the lunar mission and the question of her son were breaking her head simultaneously.

The lunar mission was destined to be launched soon. As a junior engineer, she just knew that the mission is going to be of help to the meteorological department.

She was looking into the rockets, and she couldn't resist exploring them. She walked past the rooms and touched the rockets. She pushed aside the men in-charge of security, and walked fast to enter a rocket.

Riah entered into the rocket and turned it on. The rocket flew fast up into the sky. She commanded it to move to mars crossing the earth. The lunar mission was still on her head and the pending works were disturbing her. Riah thought that she had escaped from the earth and all her works. As she was travelling in the rocket she got worried. She wondered how would she face the earth on returning. She wanted to crash the rocket into mars, but she thought of her son and her family. The rocket entered mars, and her leg was about to burn as the heat was unbearable. Riah wanted to answer Pranith, "Dear, the heat here is unbearable than our earth"."So, we must think of making the earth sustainable instead of wondering if God would show the way to mars."

Riah slipped the coffee in her hand, and she realized that she couldn't bear the heat of the spilt coffee on her leg.

Riah breathed a sigh of relief on realizing that it was a dream. The pressure of her work made her take a nap. The questions on her head and the desires of her heart led to such a dream. Riah realized that she got an answer to the question asked by Pranith. She wished that she should say about her dream of entering into mars to Pranith. She felt that both of them could have a good laugh in the evening, and she could impart a valuable lesson on sustainability to Pranith.

Riah went to the restroom and cleaned up the mess on her shawl and her leg. As she walked out crossing the security she smiled thinking about her dream. She walked to her desk and sat back to complete her pending works. Her finger typed Mars instead of the moon and the Mars mission instead of the lunar mission in most places.

It was past 4:00 P.M. Riah walked into the chief engineer's room. She wanted to submit the work desperately. She handed over a few printed documents and sent a mail about the lunar mission.

The chief engineer checked them and said, "*Riah, I think you are desperate about a mission to Mars*"."*Let that be our next agenda, but now we have to complete the lunar mission.*" Riah realized that she had not rectified her errors before submitting the document." Riah realized her mistakes. She opened the file and clicked control+F and typed mars, and on the replace space she clicked moon.

The chief engineer cracked a joke at this point. He asked."*Riah, so, now you want to replace the place of moon and Mars?".*" *I guess you can travel into space and move the mars and moon*". Riah smiled understanding his sarcasm. Riah apologized knowing that she must hear a piece of advice.

The chief engineer appreciated Riah for her good work to her surprise. He said, "*To err is to human, I understand you are engrossed with the question of your son*".To her surprise, he said, "*Riah, even I had crossed all the stages in my life, and I have made worse errors.*" He also asked, "*Why did your son ask about mars?*" Riah told about the project given to her son. The chief engineer said, "*Riah, I feel schools should make the children work on the field instead of giving written works so that children will think of sustainable development.*" Before Riah left he said, "*Tell your son that God will not show a way to mars until you make the earth sustainable*". Riah left the room with a smile.

Riah went back to her cabin. She cleared up her desk. Her mind was much clear when she left home.

Pranith had entered the home before her. She made him a yummy snack, and taught him about the ways to make the earth sustainable. She shared about her dream and the talk with her chief engineer. Pranith laughed on hearing all that, and went to his room to do his assignments. Riah relaxed in the living room, and opened her laptop to complete her pending works.

======

2.Mottalu and Pattalu

There lived crows named Mottalu and Pattalu on the trees of a busy street. Mottalu and pattalu were very close friends. One day Mottalu saw pattalu and asked" *Why are we crows, why can't we be humans, dogs, parrots, peacocks or any other animal or birds that are valued?".*

Pattalu said, "Motta, *do you know? My mom use to say this;"* God *created the world, birds, trees, animals and everything on this earth?"*

Mottalu asked, "*Are you sure everything on this earth was created by God?*

Pattalu said, "*Mom said*".

As Mottalu and Pattalu were talking with each other, an aeroplane flew fast. They stopped the conversation due to the noise made by the aeroplane. The aeroplane flew past them, and the noise was stopped.

Mottalu saw pattalu with a question mark on its face. Mottalu asked, "*Pattalu, Did God make the aeroplane, cars, bikes and trains that humans travel?".* Pattalu said with a smile," *Don't you know the answer to this question?.* Mottalu said," *Of course, humans made them for their comfort?"*

Pattalu said," Now think, aren't we gifted to be a crow?" Mottalu thought for a while. It asked, "Why are we gifted?"

They flew from one tree to another and sat back. After a few minutes, Mottalu said that it was hungry. Pattalu said," Now see we will certainly get food," Aren't we gifted?"

Mottalu said,"Pattalu, we must fly from one tree to other to get food."We must look into the terrace of the houses"."We eat the leftovers, how come it is a gift?"

Pattalu said, "We aren't eating the leftover food"." We get a chance to eat whatever we need," Please, think in a positive note". Mottalu smiled and said,"Yeah pattalu, one day I happen to see white rice. I was about to eat it and saw chicken pieces in another home. I just had a little rice and flew to eat the chicken. Pattalu asked," Are you telling me about the small piece of chicken you gave me the other day?".Mottalu said,"Yes, But it was so yummy that I had

5 and got reminded of you .Pattalu said, "Thankfully you thought of me, or else I would have said that you had lost the very nature of being a crow".

Pattalu said, "Now I understand that God creates each species for a reason, and so he created us".

Mottalu and Pattalu were talking about humans worshipping crows as ancestors. They were glad that sometimes humans give them delicious food and not the leftover for them.

They saw a mother and child on a terrace of a home. Mother was feeding the child. Mother was teaching the child that crow shares the food with other crows. Mother said to the child that we must learn the habit of sharing from crows.

Mottalu asked pattallu, "Isn't it wonderful that humans praise us for our nature". Pattalu said," Yes, But if we go and eat from that plate we will be chased". Look at the humans they are gifted. They cook and eat.

Mottalu asked pattalu," You said we are gifted". Mottalu said, "Yes, But on seeing humans I do get jealous". See they make aeroplanes and all inventions. You know these humans have something called mobiles, and they spent 24/7 with that. These humans create things beyond what God had created, but we don't create anything".

They talked about humans destroying nature. The mother kept the left over rice on the corner of the terrace and went. Pattalu said," *Look, the mother had kept the rice for us*". We need to wait until given so we won't be chased". Mottalu said let's call our other friends and have the rice. Pataalu said yes!

Pattalu and Mottalu were eating the rice, and they took a few scoops of rice and flew to share with the other crows.

Riah waited for Pranith to swallow that last scoop of rice. Thus, she ended her story of Mottalu and Pattalu by saying that crows teach a lot of valuable lessons, and every living species exist for a reason. She was glad that she had answered the question, "Why god create crows, they are just black and don't chirp melodiously like a sparrow or other birds?"

Finally, Pranith swallowed the rice. He asked," *So, Is this why crows exist?" To eat our leftover foods"* Riah smiled and said," *Yes Pranith, they help in zero wastage of valuable resource called as food".* Pranith said," *So, here after I will keep the left-over food at the terrace. I will not throw in the garbage".*

=====

3. SPEAKING TREE

Riah completed her office works.She breathed a sigh of relief. She washed the dishes in the basin, and walked to bed.

Her 5-year-old Pranith was busy with his ipad. Riah couldn't resist her anger. She expressed her anger to her adorable son.

Riah walked fast near him, and snatched the ipad from his hand. As Pranith was expressing the shock in his cute face she yelled," Could you please sleep. Am tired?" Pranith couldn't control his fear and tears after being yelled at.

Pranith spoke with innocence," *Amma, you are busy with your laptop and mobiles, and dad is also busy with his laptop and mobiles. I don't have anyone to play with, and you scold me when I play with which you bought and gave me to play."*

Riah felt guilty after hearing the innocent sentences that came along with the tears in a voice. It melted her heart.

Riah felt that she had to apologize. Riah said with a smile," *Sorry, but you should sleep soon. You have to get up fast and go to school tomorrow."*

Pranith spoke with innocence again." *Amma. If you want me to sleep now; call dad;I must talk with him for 10 minutes".*

Riah said,"*Dad is busy with work, you can play with him on Sunday".*

Pranith couldn't control his childish impulsivity. He jumped down from the bed. He ran to his dad before Riah could stop him.

Appa," *I am going to tell you one thing. I saw a speaking tree."*

Rohan stopped typing on his keyboard. He looked at him with a smile. Riah wondered what Pranith is about to talk about.

Pranith said," *Appa, give me 10 minutes, I will tell you about the speaking tree.*

Riah was also curious to know what his son meant.

Riah asked," *Ok, darling, where did you see the speaking tree?*

Pranith replied, "*In our apartment".*

Rohan forgot his official works and got engrossed. He asked," *Where in our apartment?"*

Pranith said," *In the park?"*

Rohan asked," *what did the tree speak"?*

Pranith said, "*Tree said, dad and mom will play with you every day".*

Riah and Rohan understood what the innocent heart of their son wanted.

Riah asked," *Tree said this or you want mom and dad to play with you every day".*

Pranith said," *I wanted, I said to the tree as you never listened, and the tree said that you will play with me every day".*

Riah realized her mistakes. She understood that Pranith wouldn't spend time on his tab if she and Rohan play with him.

Riah asked," *Ok, what else did the tree say?*"

Pranit said," *Tree said that humans never care for it, but they want it to save them from sun.*"

Pranith talked with his innocent sense of humour. He said, "*Tree said, "Your dad instructed you to put the chocolate cover in the garbage bin right, but yesterday he dropped a plastic bottle near me out of frustration.*"

Rohan realized that he did that during the morning while walking with Pranith. Rohan crushed and threw a bottle after receiving a call regarding the mistake he made in his work.

Rohan replied," *Pranith, tell the tree that my dad is sorry for that, and he will not throw wastes on the ground*".

Riah and Rohan were amazed by the mature talks of the innocent mind. They realized that their son watches them, and they have to be a good role model for him.

======

4. THE TOWN OF ALWIN AND HAEWIN

There lived a peacock named Helen in the town of Alwin. The people of Alwin loved it and enjoyed the dance it did during the rain.

Helen loves to dance, and she use to wait for the rain. The people of Alwin harvested the corps and used it to feed themselves. They never polluted the town. They were so friendly to the peacock. They never used firecrackers even during festivals.

The town of Alwin was full of greenery, and it was chill. It rained quite often, and Helen danced.

The people enjoyed the mountains, rivers and lakes of Alwin. As most people of Alwin enjoyed the dance of Helen and the greenery, some were bored and tired of keeping the town clean.

There was a naughty boy called Rohan in the town of Alwin. He was bored of keeping the town clean, and not bursting crackers during the festivals. He had a few naughty friends.

One day he gathered all his friends and made all of them drop all the chocolate wrappers on the streets. He wanted to enjoy bursting crackers.

There was a town called Haewin near Alwin. Haewin was not like Alwin. It was very dirty, and there were no beautiful birds.

Rohan always wished to stay in Haewin and enjoy his life. One day he and his friends went to Haewin, and got some crackers. They dirtied Alwin by bursting crackers and enjoyed their life. They never cared about the advice of the elders.

As they made the city unclean, the others in the town had a tough time cleaning it. The parents of Rohan and his friends were also scolded because they did not care to teach good values to their children.

Rohan's dad decided to teach him a lesson. He took away all the pocket money that he gave for Rohan, and the parents of his friends did the same.

Rohan and his friends never had the money for buying crackers and chocolates. So, they were sad.

They stopped making Alwin dirty. Alwin became cleaner.

Rohan called his friends and he decided to make a plan. He called his friends and said," *The people of Alwin keep the town clean so that Helen enjoy the greenery and dance for the rain. can we kill it?"*

One of his friends said," *no, we will kidnap it and put it somewhere in Haewin".*

Rohan said kidnapping is hard, but killing with a knife is easy.

Rohan said, *"Let's take a knife when everyone sleeps at home, and go to the foothills to kill it."*His friends accepted the idea of Rohan.

It was midnight. Rohan and his friends walked silently to the foothills with the knife.

They couldn't see Helen in the darkness. Suddenly, they were pushed down. They looked up. God came in the peacock. He pushed them to save Helen and the town of Alwin.

God said, *"I will break your hands and leg if you make Alwin dirty. I will kill you if you kill Helen."*

Rohan and his friends got scared and ran back to their homes. They realized their mistake.

They asked a question to god, *"The people of Haewin keep their town dirty, won't they be punished?."*

God said, *"I will punish them at the right time, wait and watch."*

Months and years went fast.

People of Alwin were healthy because the harvest was good and they kept the city clean.

It didn't rain for many months in Haewin. The crops got dried and people suffered without food. Haewin started to stink, and people fell sick.

Many people started coming to Alwin for food. They promised that they won't make Alwin dirty. But, the people of Alwin did not believe them. They didn't let them enter. The people of Alwin told them to clean the garbage at Haewin. It was a hard job because the garbage wasn't cleaned every day.

Rohan and his friends realized that God had punished them.

Rohan and his friends told the elders of Alwin that 2 years back God came in a peacock and said that he will punish the people of Haewin.

Rohan said," *God also said that he will break our legs and hands if we dirty Alwin*".

The people of Alwin were shocked. One old man asked," *So, that is why you and your friends stopped dirtying Alwin*".

They nodded.

It rained when they were talking, and Helen danced. Rohan and his friends danced along with Helen.

They accepted that they wanted to kill Helen, and that is when God came and scared them.

They said, "*God said that he will punish the people of Haewin, and he did*".

The town of Haewin was barren. People died of sickness and hunger.

======

5. THE END GAME-ROBOTS SURVIVE

It is 2100. The chirps of birds aren't heard. The breeze isn't gentle.

Various parts of the world suffered due to food shortages between the years 2089 to 2099. Those who had plants in homes used them cautiously for daily needs.

Mr Harnish was reminiscing the days when their smart home was an agricultural land once. He thought of the days when he watched the sunset and enjoyed the chirp of birds with his family.

He was watching the news on his smart screen. He was in delight as he heard,

Indoor and terrace gardening has been made compulsory by the Indian government. The government will provide needed materials to encourage the practice.

He wanted to share this with his grandson named Nirosh.

Their lawn is fitted with devices to set the water level for plants. Nirosh set the level and instructed their robot to water the plants.

As the Robot was doing its job, Nirosh saw his grandpa walking towards him with joy.

His grandpa showed the news. Nirosh thanked his grandpa for influencing their family to grow plants. He was happy that the government will provide cash for the best yields.

After discussing gardening, Nirosh said that he has instructed their robot to fetch tea from the robotic kitchen.

Mr Harnish held Nirosh's hand and said," Can we walk to the kitchen and take the cups?"

Nirosh said," Grandpa it's fun to instruct the robot.

Mr Harnish said," I behaved the same in 2025 when my parents got a smart box which Could operate all the smart devices" He quipped, "as the world functions with artificial intelligence humans lose intelligence"

As they were interacting, the robot fetched the tea to their table on the lawn.

Mr Harnish continued to watch the news.

Nirosh opened his school tab and found the assignment "environmental degradation over the century" is to be submitted soon.

He instructed the robot to give information.

His robot continued to provide information. It showed the images of green lands and water resources that were exploited. It showed the details of calamities around the world in the century.

There was a sudden tremor. The tea fell on his tab.

Nirosh was shocked as there wasn't any intimation from the metrological department.

Soon, people around the world shared their experiences through social media. They blamed the experts for negligence to detect before the occurrence.

The experts said they were bewildered, but there would be calamities in future without intimation.

It is 2150!

Nirosh was reminiscing the days he spent with his grandparents. He was sharing the history of farming with his son.

Suddenly, there was an earthquake. The ocean expressed its anger without intimation.

Humans couldn't survive for long without nutritious food.

It is 2200!

The Self-recharged solar-powered robots survived the calamities for years. They enjoyed the sun till it shined. They missed the humans who created them

======

EARTH'S LOYAL FRIEND- 5 Stories to teach sustainability

The stories in this book are to teach the concept of sustainability in the simple way for the kids. The stories would make the children think on saving the earth for the future. Parents hold the responsibility of teaching the children on the importance of caring for the earth. Read these stories and let the children interpret the stories on their own. Let the children ask as much as questions as possible and their inquisitive nature will ignite the adults and children.

www.ingramcontent.com/pod-product-compliance
Lightning Source LLC
Chambersburg PA
CBHW020857160726
47993CB00004B/1694